W9-AGC-767

THE MASK
OF THE
DANCING PRINCESS

This book is for Eva Friedlander and Kirk Ferguson,
with special thanks to Barbara and Frank Dosne
for technical help and spiritual cheer.

THE MASK OF THE
DANCING PRINCESS

written and illustrated by

Judith Gwyn Brown

ATHENEUM   1989   NEW YORK

There was once in the land of Valleria a king who had an only daughter. On the hour the princess was born, the queen died, and the child, named after her, was called Rosamond. The king loved the baby dearly, and every night, as he watched her sleep in her cradle, his eyes filled with tenderness.

During the day the king sat on his great throne, making just and good laws for his people. Because his time was taken so much this way, the princess grew up without a mother's kiss and with only servants to attend her. She took her first steps through the long halls and gardens of the palace alone or with strangers, and now that she was almost ten years old, though she had golden hair and graceful ways, she was, alas, unkind.

She would not smile at anyone nor speak to anyone as a friend, so haughty and proud was she. None of the gifts her father, the king, gave her pleased her: neither the talking bird who called her name nor the tiny teahouse built in the garden of the palace. When she received these gifts Rosamond gave no thanks, but turned away.

Because of her unkindness, the king was in deep sorrow. One night, a month before Rosamond's tenth birthday, he stood at the foot of her bed and watched his child sleep. Thinking she could not hear him, he murmured to himself aloud, "Someday I will die, and the kingdom will be ruled by Rosamond, but she is so unkind and has so little imagination of the heart she will not be worthy to rule the land."

Yet the king was a doting father, and the next day he asked his daughter what birthday present she would have.

"I will have nothing," said the princess, "but a child to attend me who is exactly like myself. A child who looks like me and speaks like me, and has the face I see in my glass in every way."

The king shook his head. "That is impossible," he said. "I could never find anyone like you, my dear daughter. On the day of your birth you were the only babe born to your poor mother."

The princess stamped her foot. "I will have what I wish or I will never speak to you again. Then you'll be sorry," she said, and sweeping up her skirts, she left the room.

The king sighed. "Woe to my kingdom when Rosamond sits upon the throne and rules the land."

But the king loved his daughter and called his counselors to him. He told them that they must search the kingdom to find a child who looked and talked and walked exactly like the Princess Rosamond.

The next day the lord counselor, Swallowstripe, marched out with four of his men. They visited the great houses of marble and stone wherein lived gentlemen of rank and riches, and they entered fine galleries deep-carpeted and hung with curtains of velvet and silk. The king's men bowed stiffly to the little girls who were brought to stand in a row before them. Lord Swallowstripe wrote down in a large book which child had the eyes of the princess, and which had the color of her glorious golden hair. Against this he also noted where each child failed to resemble the Princess Rosamond in height or bearing or tint of cheek.

Then the king's men marched into the city and towns. They visited the neat brick homes of merchants, shopkeepers, and shoemakers. Lord Swallowstripe was offered the best chair in the parlor, and he sat with his book and looked upon the pretty girls who wore their best party dresses and stood before him. Not one of the daughters here looked exactly like the Princess Rosamond.

The day after this the king's men tramped through the countryside, passing barns and haylofts. Swallowstripe entered farmhouses and stood in the

kitchen with his book. Here girls ten years of age were sent before the king's men, and they came dressed in gingham, giggling and bobbing up and down, carrying brooms and baby brothers.

Swallowstripe wrote down that no one here resembled the Princess Rosamond at all.

As the king's men journeyed back to the palace they rested near an open meadow where a band of wandering players was setting up camp. These were the dancing actors who traveled from place to place, country to country—the Droll Mummers of the World. The king's men watched as the players raised their tents and practiced their art.

There were jugglers and actors and dancers and a trained bear. The lord counselor followed one little dancer with his eyes, a young girl with hair the color of a raven's wing.

She took her steps cleverly with brown, bare feet as her black hair tumbled over her face. She did not look like the king's daughter, but she was quick and clever and stamped her feet to the rhythm of the dance.

As Lord Swallowstripe gazed on the actors before him, the leader of the troupe came up to him. He said his name was Reynaldo and bowed low with a sidelong glance and a smile that showed a gold tooth.

He offered Swallowstripe the card of his business. The king's counselor took the card and read:

> *Dancers and Players and Jugglers are we.*
> *We sing and we dance for a modest fee.*
> *Droll Mummers, Masked Drummers, Wanderers free.*
> *Traveling Actors and Gypsies. Come see!*

Swallowstripe put the card between the pages of his book, and he and his men continued on their way.

The next day when the lord counselor returned to the palace without a child who looked like the princess, the king bit his lip and pulled at his beard. He begged Princess Rosamond to choose something else for her birthday, but the royal child only shook her head, shut the door to her room with a bang, and would speak to no one.

The king sat up all night with Lord Swallowstripe reading through his book of names: the names of little girls who almost looked like the princess—almost, but not exactly so. The two men thought deeply as the candle before them gutted into its wick. Just before dawn the lord counselor had an idea. He closed his great book with a thud and bent over to whisper in the king's ear.

At first the king shook his head no, and again no; but as the early-morning light came into the room, he agreed to the lord counselor's plan.

Shortly after dawn the king went to his daughter's room, and standing outside the locked door, he told her that her wish had been granted. A child had been found who looked like her in every way, and on her birthday this child would be presented before her.

That morning the king gave commands to the workmen in the castle. They were ordered to toil day and night, to build within the great hall of the palace a small theater, the oak door of which would be kept locked by a silver key. And build it they did. For three weeks the palace halls echoed with the sound and din of scraping and sawing and nailing of wood. The theater had a gleaming stage for the actors, and surrounding the shining platform on three sides was a balcony decorated with winged babies playing on harps and horns. The seats were of plum velvet, and the curtain that hung over the polished boards was cloth of gold. Silk streamers made a tent above the stage, and the hall would be lit by flickering candlelight.

When the king saw that it was finished, he locked the door, put the key in his treasure chest, and looked upon what he had done with a heavy heart.

On the afternoon of the princess's birthday she was dressed in white, with silk embroidered slippers on her feet. A party was given in the garden on the great lawn. There were games and sweets, favors and masks, and the children of high degree from nearby kingdoms came to wish the royal child a happy day. They each brought a gift to Rosamond; a present or a toy, marvelous indeed, according to the size and wealth of their land.

The Grand Duke of Oliphant, who was only seven, presented to the princess a tiny cannon that would set off a cloud of fireworks that sparkled and flashed like colored jewels.

The Lady Henrietta gave her a china figure in the shape of a flowering bush. When the princess turned a key on one side, she could smell every rare perfume that had ever been made.

10

Through the afternoon, packages and parcels were offered the princess, but she smiled at nothing. At last Prince Edward of Wayland came forward with his present in his hands. The prince was fifteen years old and had once seen Rosamond's picture. He was so taken by her beauty that he had made the gift himself. It was a model of a seagoing ship that was built of acorns and carved woods. With a proud shyness, he set it before her.

When the princess saw the ship of wood, she did not take it up, but looked down at Edward as if he were an insect on a branch, and turned away.

Prince Edward Roderick George tripped over his feet and grew red in the cheeks. But he watched Rosamond's long hair float and curl in the springtime breeze; he saw her eyes gray as the morning mist and thought she was the most beautiful creature he had ever seen. Backing away from the royal child's presence, he stumbled over a chair and blushed in misery because his heart was touched. He felt that he would never be the same, and all afternoon, standing under the dim shade of a tree, he watched the princess. Hiding among the leaves, he told himself he would join his country's army and die in battle.

Someone else watched the princess that afternoon, hiding behind the hedges of the garden. It was Maria, the dancing girl of the Droll Mummers.

At ten o'clock that evening the Princess Rosamond sat in her place in the little theater. She was surrounded by the lords and ladies of the court. She would not bend and speak with them, but she held up a mask to her face and thought only of the gift that was to come. The entertainment began in front of the gold curtain. The audience clapped as jugglers and a trained bear performed and musicians played on fiddles and bells.

At last the curtain was drawn up. The scene before the princess was of a tower in the forest. The princess saw a girl of her own age seated on top of the tower, a child who looked just like herself. She wore the same white gown and combed the same long, golden hair. As she sat on the tower top, the child gazed upon a looking glass and talked to the image she saw there. Then the little girl ran dancing down the steps of the tower and talked to the birds that circled about her, twittering like musical flutes. The child danced on. She tiptoed to a stream of water. Bending over it with her yellow hair, she was so enchanted with the creature in the stream that she tried to touch it, but when she did, the face disappeared into the ripples and she wept. The child danced on, stepping through the cardboard forest searching, searching. At last she stopped. She looked across the light of the stage and saw the princess sitting in her gilded chair. Springing up, she whirled on her toes, shaded her eyes, and peered at the royal child. She stood just behind the footlights and put up her hands to her mouth as if to call. Then she waved to the princess and jumped up, singing out, "Here I am! Here I am!" She opened her arms wide and high with delight. Then, as the music swelled, she spun about faster and faster. Bells and drums and horns played loud and clear in triumph. The little dancer bowed low before the princess, and the music thundered as the golden curtain was let down.

It was over. The lords and ladies stood up and clapped their hands. They threw tiny bouquets of flowers upon the stage as the light went on in the little theater.

The clock struck the midnight hour. Princess Rosamond got up from her chair. She turned to the king.

"Father," she said, "I would speak to the child who is like myself."

"No," answered the king, "your birthday is over. You have had your wish. The dawn of this morning will start an ordinary day." He rose heavily from his chair, and he moved to the door with his men. The ladies-in-waiting took Princess Rosamond to her room, and soon the little theater was dark and empty.

Rosamond was too excited to go to bed. She could feel her heart beat inside her. She waited until all was quiet, and then she picked up a candle and

left the room. She walked through the long, shadowy corridors of the palace; she glided through the halls, down the staircase past the gallery until she was in the little theater again.

The princess climbed onto the stage. She parted the curtain and went behind it. Far in one corner she saw a light burning in a tiny room. She walked slowly toward the light and stood looking through the doorway. In the room was a table with a mirror, and before the table was a chair and a Japanese screen. In a traveling trunk near the screen, the princess saw strange hats and wigs of hair, stiff gowns of taffeta, and shawls of gauze and net.

Suddenly from behind the screen the little dancer appeared and stood before the princess. Rosamond felt as though she were looking at herself in a glass. The girl was exactly as tall as she and had the same long, yellow hair; her lips were as red and her cheeks were as pale. She was dressed as the princess, in purest white.

"Who are you?" demanded the princess. "Speak!" she cried.

The child put her finger to her lips and said nothing. Then the dancing girl laughed with a sound the princess knew to be her own. She pulled from her traveling trunk a scarf of red silk with tiny coins and placed it over the princess's head, covering Rosamond's hair in a veil of scarlet. Taking her by the hand, she led the royal child onto the dimly lit stage. They walked among the cardboard trees and up the steps to the top of the tower.

There the princess stopped and seized the girl's arm and tightened her fingers about it.

"You will be my friend always," she said. "You will live here in the palace and do all the things I wish, and since we are alike and the same, it will be everything you wish, too. We will have secrets and play tricks and…"

The dancing girl shook her head. "I cannot live in the palace," she said.

"I command it," said the princess. "You will!"

"No," said the girl in a low voice, "I cannot, for I must travel with my people, who need me."

"You will do as I say," cried the princess, "for you are me." She grabbed the girl and shook her, and she pulled at the long, yellow hair, which was so much like her own. The princess looked into the girl's eyes, and suddenly they were not like her own, for they were wild and dark, and the princess could see that beneath the pale paint on her face a darker color shone. She clutched at the golden hair and saw it twist over the girl's cheek, like a rag, for it was only a wig. Everything was false—eyes and face and hair. All was unreal. All was paint and make-believe and falseness.

The dancing girl stepped back, her eyes wide with fear. Back she stepped toward the tower edge. The princess heard a crack of wood, a splitting, splintering sound. The tower rim gave way and the girl cried out. Rosamond watched as with a crash the child fell through the false trees to the polished boards below.

The princess stood still and could not move. No cry came from the child. Only silence. Then Rosamond ran as swiftly as she could down the steps of the tower. Her world was spinning, and the blood pounded in her head like a drum. In the hall there was a deathlike quiet.

"Maria, Maria, where are you?" the princess heard someone call in the darkened theater. Through the shadows a man and a woman appeared. They climbed over the balcony onto the little stage. They looked at the princess in the scarlet veil bending over the child who lay still as death on the floor before them.

"Maria!" shrieked the woman of the Droll Mummers. "You have killed the royal princess. The king will kill us all for this."

The man picked up the limp body of the child from the floor, and the woman snatched Rosamond by the hand and dragged her through the back hallways of the palace to a cobblestone yard. The princess was thrust roughly into a wooden cart with the still body of the dancing girl. She was choked with horror at what she had done and what would be done to her. Quickly the man and woman climbed onto the seat of the wagon and they started off.

Outside the town stood the Droll Mummers' camp. Tents and caravans, animals and carts stood in the blackness of night. There the gypsy man called out, waking everyone, shouting that Maria had killed the king's daughter and that they all must flee. The Droll Mummers swiftly pulled down their tents,

hitched up the caravans, and followed the wagon. Eight caravans moved as one long running animal down the streak of road into darkness. The gypsy men cracked their whips and shouted to their horses, driving them recklessly. The moon came out from behind the clouds as they plunged over the hills, speeding in flight to a new land.

In the wagon the princess huddled next to the dancing child. She clutched the still form in terror and wept hot tears until the moon seemed to break into a thousand pieces, and the tears on her face felt like blood.

The wagon lurched against a rock and the princess heard a moan. The child, Maria, was alive. The princess called out to the driver to stop, but her cries mingled with the wind and the shouts of the frightened players and the beat of the horses' hooves. They drove on all night long.

In the morning the caravan came to a halt. The player gypsies looked in the wagon and saw Rosamond with the child Maria in her arms. At last the Droll Mummers realized their mistake. In terror they took Maria and put her in another caravan with an old woman, Abishag, who would nurse her, and they continued on their way. The princess rode on alone as the wagons rolled and reeled over mudlands and hills.

After many days, the leader, Reynaldo, held up his hand and the horses were pulled to a stop. "Here we will stay for a while," he said.

The dark players untied the horses and set up camp. They talked among themselves, and one said they must kill the princess or they would all be killed. Another said that they should send her back to the king. But Reynaldo the leader said, "No." They could not trust great ones unless they had given their word sworn on their honor. The princess should be kept in a cage and a dog be set to guard her.

So the princess was put into a cage that was made of black wood held fast with nails. It had iron bars on two sides, for it was a cage that had been used to keep animals. A spotted dog called Topaz was chained outside all day and put into the cage at night to make sure she did not escape. The princess sat still as death, staring at the bars that enclosed her. The old woman, Abishag, brought some straw for her to sleep on, and Maria was sent to bring her food.

Every morning Maria pushed open the door to the cage and slid a bowl of beans, bread, and a cup of goat's milk to the princess. Rosamond gazed upon her and would not speak, but Maria stood before the cage and looked at her through the bars with pity, and when she could, she added a handful of berries or a bit of cheese to the bowl. The little dancer was sorry she had brought such a burden of misfortune to the royal child and to her own tribe.

In the meanwhile, the king and his men searched everywhere for the princess but could not find her. The king sat on his throne, his head in his hands, and was sad beyond comfort. Mourning his daughter, whom he believed to be dead, he shut the door of the little theater and locked it, leaving all to dust and cobwebs within.

A month passed and Rosamond felt a great emptiness in her heart. Through the bars of the cage, she watched the Droll Mummers all day long. She saw them tend their horses and goats, repair their caravans, fetch water from the streams, and gather wood for the fire. She sat in her cage of darkness as if it were a cave and looked out through the bars, watching her captors eat and drink and sometimes laugh. And in the evenings she watched them dance and play for the people who came from the neighboring towns to see them perform.

In the distance the firelight was bright. As the hours passed into the deep chill of night, before the gypsies retired to their caravans, the spotted dog was put into her cage. The royal child, in her great sorrow and loneliness, reached out her hand to the dog and buried her head in the animal's thick, rough fur. She warmed herself against Topaz's spotted belly and cried until she fell asleep.

When it became high summer, the gypsy players traveled northward. They took the princess with them, placing the cage on a wagon, and moved on until they reached a deep forest. Once again they argued about what they might do with the child and some said one thing, and some said another, but they could not agree.

The next day, when she brought food, Maria whispered to the princess, "The elders are talking, and some would see that you lose your way in the forest, and some would keep you locked in the cage forever. Indeed, I'm sorry for all that has happened—for you and for us. And I've been thinking; if you will learn to dance for the strangers as I do, my people might let you free for a little time every night. Swear on your honor as a royal child that you will not run from me, and I will teach you what you need to know." The princess nodded: Yes.

At noontime, when all the camp was at rest, and no one stirred in the heat of the day, Maria took an iron key from beneath a rock and opened the cage. Rosamond crawled forward and, holding onto the bars, began to get up. So stiff and cold had her limbs become that when she stood at first, the ground seemed to shift beneath her. At last she was able to put one foot before the other. Maria beckoned to the princess, and the two girls climbed up one hill and then another so no one would see them. There Maria, holding a small drum, beat out a slow rhythm and showed Rosamond the first step of a dance.

25

The princess pointed her toe in her silk slippers that were now torn and soiled. She put out her foot as she thought Maria had done, but it was all wrong. And Maria said so. Rosamond tried again, but it was still wrong. Maria grew frightened and said, "If you don't learn to dance for them, they will chain you up again, and I will be beaten for trying to help you."

A cold chill passed through Rosamond, and she shivered in the hot sun of noon. She bent down and pulled off her silk slippers and, throwing them from her, stood barefoot on the earth.

When the gypsy girl hit the little drum again, the princess tried with all her might to do what she was told with her hands and feet. She learned to step, point, tap, turn, clap her hands, and stamp her feet. And when Maria shook her head, Rosamond tried again and again. Every noon as the Droll Mummers slept, Maria took Rosamond into the forest and taught her the steps that would keep her alive. Slowly the princess learned one dance and then another as Maria coaxed and scolded and praised. After many weeks Maria said proudly, "Soon you can be one of us."

The next day, when Maria came to fetch the princess, she carried with her a box bound in leather, held closed by buckles. It was heavy and Maria felt its weight as she led the princess through the forest, up a high hillside to a meadow with a running stream.

There she opened the box and took out a small mirror, a china bowl, and a bottle of black liquid. She filled the bowl with inky dye and dipped the princess's golden hair into it. The princess's long hair turned black as a raven's wing, black as the darkest night, black as Maria's own. Then the girl of the Droll Mummers took from the box pots of paint and colored powders and brushes for making up. There was red rouge for lips and cheeks, blue salve for shadows about the eyes, and black and brown pencils for eyelashes and brows.

Maria put these out on a rock and set to work painting the princess's face. She painted Rosamond with the face of a child of the out-of-doors, tawny brown from the sun, with ruddy cheeks. Then she painted Rosamond's eyes

like a dancer's eyes, with a line of black about the rim. When she had done this, Maria took from the box a bundle of cloths of purple and orange, blue and green. She dressed the princess in skirts and veils of color, and she decorated her with bangles that looked like silver and gold. The gypsy girl stood back and was pleased with what she had done, and she bid Rosamond look into a small mirror. The princess looked into it and was amazed.

Maria said, "Now you will be one of us, and we will be friends forever." And she laughed with joy and grabbed Rosamond's hand. And the two, holding hands tight, swung with their arms out full length, dancing round and round in a blur of rushing leaves and bright midday sun.

When they returned to the caravans, Maria took Rosamond up to the old woman, Abishag, who seemed a bundle of black rags stirring a pot over a smoky fire. Maria told Abishag what she had done, and the old woman peered up close at the princess. Then, putting a hand to her own withered face, she touched Rosamond's mouth with a bony finger. "Now you must learn to smile," she said.

Then the old woman taught Rosamond to look up and smile at strangers as if she were a small child; to give a sidelong glance and smile like a gypsy dancer; to look down and smile like a beggar maid. All of these smiles were to please the strangers so they would put silver coins in the palm of the old woman sitting in the firelight.

That evening, during the Droll Mummers' council, Abishag spoke up for the princess and said that she ought to earn her bread, that Maria had taught her to dance, and that, since she was so far from her own country, there would be no danger to the tribe. After some talk, Reynaldo the leader agreed. So the princess painted her face every night and danced and smiled; and the strangers clapped to the rhythm of her feet and put silver in the wrinkled palm of Abishag. And the gypsy players traveled a long way, over many miles, and the princess traveled with them and shared the fortunes of the year.

When it was summer and the hot sun blazed down, Rosamond had to carry buckets of water from the stream, clean out the animals' pens, and go with Abishag into the villages where the old woman bargained for food, and where the princess was told to lower her head and smile so they would get more for their penny.

When the rains rained down and no one came to the tents for the dancing, and mud filled the roads, the Droll Mummers huddled in their caravans. Water poured down and seeped through the roofs of their shelters as birds and mice drowned in the fields. The wandering tribe had little to eat, and Rosamond and Maria shared what they had with Topaz, though they often went hungry themselves.

But when the times were good and the weather friendly, Rosamond and Maria climbed up into the hills with the goats that they took to graze there. Sometimes the dancing bear followed them like a dog, and Topaz raced on ahead. The two girls picked mint and wildflowers to sell and looked down on the villages and towns far below. They knew they could not belong to the people there, but they were glad to be on the sunny hill with the animals, together.

In the years that followed, Maria taught Rosamond to laugh and sing as well as dance, and Rosamond taught Maria to read and write and speak like the ladies of the court. And Abishag watched over them as she sewed, chanting and crooning the stories and tales of her youth.

Sometimes Rosamond thought of the days in the palace, but it was so long ago—in another land and time—almost like a dream. The caravans moved from place to place, and in this way seven years passed.

Then one day the wandering players traveled high in the mountains of Wayland, near the country of Valleria. They camped near the famous rock caves, and there it was that the Droll Mummers set up their flags. Torches blazed as people on holiday nearby came up the mountains to see their dancing and hear the music. The caves were crowded and no one took notice of a young man who sat among them watching the singers and jugglers and musicians. The young man was Prince Edward, dressed as a rider. He had been on horseback all day and had stopped to rest; and seeing the festive group, he decided to stay for the entertainment. Prince Edward often rode out this way, wearing a hat to shade his face so that he might hear what his countrymen had to say when they talked freely among themselves.

The prince sat on the ground in the dim cave by the firelight and watched the musicians who stood and sat on the other side of the flickering flame. The music began softly with flutes and bells and little drums, and then a player came forward who plucked the strings of a guitar and set them humming like an echo through the cave. Others began playing, and Edward felt a strumming, singing, thrumming inside him as the Droll Mummers, the Masked Drummers, filled the dark air with their sound.

Soon from the shadows of the cave the dancers came spinning and swirling into the firelight. The prince looked at one young dancer, and, suddenly, before he could think with his head, he felt a great leap in his heart, and the blood rose to his face. He saw that the dancer wore a red silk scarf over black hair that was streaming behind her as she spun to the rhythm of the drums. He saw that instead of looking proud, she was smiling wildly, but

he was sure the girl who wore tiny bells on her feet was the daughter of the king of Valleria, Princess Rosamond.

Edward stared at her, so overcome by what he felt that the young dancer, peering through the firelight, saw him, too.

She stopped smiling, and for a moment she looked as if she would call

out, but glancing into the dark corners of the cave, she saw something that made her pull the red scarf about her face like a veiled mask. She spun away from him, whirling into the darkness.

Prince Edward jumped up and was going to shout to her, but before him he saw a group of the player men standing watchfully in the shadows,

touching the gleaming knives that were tucked into their leather belts. The prince knew that even if he were willing to die fighting for the princess, he could not chance that she be hurt. So he threw a gold coin into the lap of the old woman who sat by the fire and ran out of the cave.

For three days the prince of Wayland rode day and night. He crossed the boundry of his own lands and galloped on through the country of Valleria, stopping only for water to drink. He was red-eyed and faint with weariness as he approached the gates of the city. There his lame horse stumbled, and the prince was thrown hard onto the rocky ground, hitting his head and falling into blackness.

The next day the soldiers who guarded the gates of the city found him and carried him, sick with fever, into the presence of the king. The horse was put into the stable and doctors came, but it was three days more before the king heard Prince Edward's story. The king was amazed at what he heard. He called his men and told them to saddle their horses and ride to the mountains in the country of Wayland to seek and find the princess. The king's men rode out that very day, but when they reached the caves, the Droll Mummers were gone, and the rocks echoed only their own angry voices.

When the men returned to the palace, the king was filled with despair as he sat in his great hall on his throne of grief. Now he felt very old, and he thought he would never see his daughter again. Great tears blinded his eyes and ran down his beard as he wept, and his heart was filled with bitterness toward the traveling players. In his rage and despair the king swore vengeance on the wandering tribe that had caused him so much pain, and he thought of a plan to trap them.

He wrote a letter and fixed it with a wax seal the color of blood and stamped it with a heavy ring. The king took the paper and sent for his scribe, who copied his words many times. Then the king's soldiers took these papers and rode out to the highways and into the kingdoms near and far. They nailed the letters to posts in the marketplace and on trees in the forest. The king's command said that if those persons who had taken the princess from the palace seven years before would return her to the king, they would be pardoned and given a bag of gold as reward.

When the Droll Mummers saw this letter nailed to a tree, they marveled at the promise it made. They could trust a king's word certainly. Could they not? Indeed, they would have a pardon; and they would have the money, too.

The princess had been a burden to them, Reynaldo said, and they were willing to give her up, but they wanted to be sure of the reward and could not take a chance on her running off. They talked among themselves and agreed that she be put back in a cage and kept there until they were inside the palace gate. Then they put the cage on a wagon, and with their horses and caravans they rode toward the kingdom of Valleria.

It was a hard journey; the wagons and carts rattled through the cold spring rains. Sometimes the caravans stuck fast in the mud of the roads, and the horses, already sore-footed and weary, were forced, straining, to pull them out.

The princess was once again a prisoner, but now Maria trudged beside the cage and spoke words of comfort through the bars that separated them. Topaz ran back and forth, barking with fear, and the caravans rode on late into the night. The Droll Mummers were bruised and dirty with the mud and dust of the roads, and they were hungry because they looked wild and no one would sell them bread. They rode through villages, where they were stoned by boys, and they traveled on the open highways, urging their horses as fast as they could go.

At last they arrived at the palace of the king of Valleria and shouted to the guard on the tower gate to let them in. A soldier blew a trumpet, and slowly the iron gate was lifted above their heads. The caravans creaked on the cobblestones of the yard and the wagons rumbled and swayed as if they would fall apart.

The king was seated on his throne in his chamber of state, and when he heard the sounds of the trumpets on the battlements, he marched with his men through the halls of the palace. He gathered his majestic robes and cloak about him, and when the great door was opened, he stood in the doorway, his white hair streaming down his shoulders.

When the caravans and wagons were inside the courtyard, the iron gate dropped shut with a bang. The Droll Mummers looked about them and saw rows of armed soldiers surrounding them, their muskets pointing straight at the carts. Frozen in fear, the women and children huddled against the wagons.

The king's voice boomed through the courtyard.

"Where is my child?" he cried.

The Droll Mummers stood still as stones. But Reynaldo unhooked the horse from the wagon on which the cage was placed. He pushed the wagon slowly before the king and, standing beside the cage, fitted a rusty key into the lock and opened it.

The king peered between the bars and he saw there a dark-haired girl and a spotted dog crowded in one corner. Slowly the girl crept through the little door and stood before him. The girl was dressed in gaudy rags and her face was streaked with dirt and she was spent with weariness from the long journey.

The king held the scepter of his office like a club. He shook his head and grew angry.

"This is not my daughter," he cried. His voice broke, and he said in a whisper no one else could hear, "My beautiful daughter had hair of gold." Then he bellowed into the courtyard, and an echo shouted back in return.

"WHERE IS MY CHILD?"

Everyone moved back in silence, but the princess stood still and said in a low voice, "Oh, Papa, don't you know me?"

"My daughter had golden hair," murmured the king, and his voice was harsh with longing.

"Papa, it's me, Rosamond. Please listen and I'll tell you true things so you'll know I'm yours. Long ago, on the night of my birthday, I left the palace."

The king shook his head sadly. "Everyone in the kingdom knows that. It takes no gypsy girl to say so."

The princess stepped forward and put out her hand to him. "On that day there was a party in the garden and—"

41

The king shook his head and said, "Everyone in the kingdom knows that. It takes no false witch to say so."

The princess said, "One night when you thought I was asleep, you whispered so I could hardly hear, 'My daughter has so little imagination of the heart she will not be worthy to rule my kingdom.' Not worthy. Not worthy ever."

The king looked at Rosamond, and tears came to his eyes and rolled down his weary, lined face, and he wept for all to see. He stepped toward her on unsteady feet and put out his arms.

"Only my child could know this and say so," he cried.

He was about to take her to his heart, when Reynaldo pushed himself before the king. The leader of the Droll Mummers smiled, holding his head to one side; a solid gold tooth showed.

"Oh, Majesty, do not doubt that this is your daughter. We have cared for her these seven years and she has eaten our bread for all that time. Surely we have earned the pardon and reward you have promised." He looked up at the king with a sidelong glance and held open his palm.

The king looked at the leader of the Droll Mummers and grew angry. And remembering his grief of seven long years, he raised his hand as a signal to the soldiers, who made ready their firearms and were about to take the gypsy band prisoners, or shoot them if they resisted.

But the princess threw herself down on the cobblestone and knelt before the king and cried, "Stop it. Stop them. I beg you. Oh, Majesty, forgive me and forgive those who have brought me here, for their life is hard, and we all need pardon for what we do. Look into your heart and imagine what it is like to have no home, to travel through the cold rains of winter and the endless dust of summer. Imagine what it is like to beg for the food you eat and to be helpless before strangers; to be at their mercy, to be at your mercy as I am now. Papa, look into your heart and think what this is like."

For a moment, the king, pale as death, closed his eyes. Then he opened them and looked at Rosamond as he used to when she slept as a babe in her cradle. He let fall the scepter, symbol of his office, and it crashed with a clatter to the ground. Then he held out his arms and gathered the princess to him, and suddenly weak, all anger gone, he murmured, "Oh, Rosamond, you are worthy. You are worthy."

He spread his wide cloak over her shoulders, and together they passed through the door of the palace and made their way, arm in arm, through the long halls to the high room of state; and none dared follow them but the spotted dog.

Leading up to the great throne were some steps, and father and daughter sat on the lowest step as Topaz stretched out in sleep at their feet. It was here that Rosamond told the king of her travels with the wandering players. And the king marveled at the hardships she had known, but he saw within her eyes a sympathy that filled him with joy.

Then he stood and raised up his child and bid her sit on the great throne of state. Taking the crown from his head, he held it high above her and made there a sign of his blessing.

The next day the king commanded a great feast in celebration of his daughter's return. But first the king gave Reynaldo his promised reward. Then, turning to Maria, he put into her hand the key that unlocked the little theater and said it was hers to use as she wished. And Maria knew the key was more precious than gold, for in that room all dreams are possible, and she held tight to the key as her thoughts flew on ahead.

Then everyone in Valleria was invited to the happy celebration, and the gypsies' music filled the air. The feast was held out-of-doors in the garden sunlight, and long tables were set out, spread with good things to eat. There were baskets of bread, tureens of soup, and covered platters of roasted meats. There were fruit and pies and cakes and cream.

Prince Edward sat beside Princess Rosamond, and between the serving of the soup and the roast, they talked of whether it is harder to build a ship of acorns and carved woods than it is to dance in the firelight. Though they talked for a long time, they could not make up their minds. Between the serving of the roast and the greens, they talked of whether it was harder to be a traveling player or a good and just prince. And though they talked for a long time, they could not make up their minds. Between the cordial and the cake, the prince asked the princess to dance. And the princess made up her mind at once: Yes.

When Edward put his arm about her waist, she did not smile as a child, nor did she smile as a wandering player, but as they danced together, her eyes shone as a summer's day, and she smiled to him as Rosamond, his own true love, bride of his heart, the bright queen of their kingdom to be.

———————————•◦•◾———————————

Copyright © 1989 by Judith Gwyn Brown

All rights reserved. No part of this book may be reproduced
or transmitted in any form or by any means, electronic or
mechanical, including photocopying, recording, or by any
information storage and retrieval system, without permission
in writing from the publisher.

Atheneum
Macmillan Publishing Company
866 Third Avenue, New York, NY 10022
Collier Macmillan Canada, Inc.
First Edition
Printed in Hong Kong

Library of Congress Cataloging-in-Publication Data
Brown, Judith Gwyn.
The mask of the dancing princess/written and illustrated by
Judith Gwyn Brown.—1st ed.   p.   cm.
Summary: Her self-centered insistence on the birthday gift of her
choice causes the young Princess Rosamond to spend seven years as an
unwilling member of a traveling band of gypsies, during which she
becomes worthy to assume the throne of her kingdom.
ISBN 0-689-31427-2
[1. Princesses—Fiction.   2. Gypsies—Fiction.   3. Conduct of
life—Fiction.]   I. Title.   PZ7.B81426Mas   1989
[E]—dc19   88–27151   CIP   AC